The Day of Delight

Tales of *fun, fantasy,*
half-truths,
myths and *fibs*

A collection of poems for
Tiddlers, Teensters, Big-Bods
and *Oldie-Pops*

By
Marian Moxham

For my grandsons,
Joshua and Jasper

First published by in Great Britain in 2022
By *Snow Beach Music and Books*

Email: **snowbeachmusicandbooks@outlook.com**

ISBN 978-1-7397798-0-1

CONTENTS

MY TORTOISE AND MY SHOUT

I've been bitten by mosquitos
Frightened by beetles
And frogs make me turn round and run
Don't talk of spiders, I'll shiver and shriek
And worms make my knee-caps turn numb!

But I love my tortoise
He's **not** slow, just cautious –
Eats greens from seeds that I grow
There are things in my garden, I'd rather not meet
But tortoise is **not** one of those!

He sleeps in the winter
And greets me months later
In spring, when the tulips come out
I'm so pleased to see him; I yell and I dance
I have plenty of reason to shout!

When I don't shriek at **this**
Well, I might huff at **that**
Auntie swears I'm vocally batty
I'll squeak when I'm scared, yes, I groan when I'm mad
And I **SHOUT** when I'm very happy!

THESE DAYS ARE HERE AGAIN

Babies wide-eyed in the sand
Crawling, *laughing*, clapping hands
Danny's *shrieking* at a crab
Tracy's *shouting* at her dad
Fairground rides and summer tides
These days are here again.

Bodies *flopped* on bathing towels
Mum's relaxed a lot more now
Sand in my sweets, not so nice!
Carefree hours and dreamy skies
Dogs are *jumping* in the surf
These days are here again.

Lots of people strolling by
A purple kite, high in the sky
Jolly games upon the sand
Donkey rides, a loud brass band
Seagulls, circle, *screech* and dive
These days are here again.

Worries gone, no work, no school
We write postcards by the pool
Our winter plans have turned to gold
Our eager dreams they now unfold

Here we are, at last, *at last...*
These days are here again.

NEW BLUE SHOES

We laughed so much, we fell on the floor, and
Charlie, our dog, bumped his head on the door
When Renee's shoe flew over the fence
    I wonder if we'll see it again?

Aiden had thrown it up in the air
    It looped-the-loop, like a plane, over there
       'Those new blue shoes should be on your feet
                Not sky-diving!'
       huffed our neighbour, Pete.

Mike took a torch, climbed over the wall
Searched in the alley, *there was no shoe!*
It was getting dark, too dark to play
    Oops, I think we lost a shoe today!

Renee's Granny was mighty mad
To tell you the truth, I did feel bad
But what can you do with a flying shoe?
    When it lands, and hides, where it chooses to!

It never appeared, not *ever* again
We looked once or twice... and then, once again
It must have gone off for a walk, on its own...
    Well, that's what I thought, as I skipped on home.

JEFFREY AND DAISY

Jeffrey Jones fell *smack* on the floor
He really couldn't stand anymore
The jumps and hops that he'd done today
Made his knees go wobbly, feet feel like clay.

Wobbly, tobbly, worn out and ah…
He wished he had a bike or a cart
With feet like clay and two wobbly knees
A bike or a cart would have helped indeed!

Little Miss Daisy sat on her wall
Singing a song since returning from school
Jeffrey Jones was heading her way
She looked, she stared, she shouted out, *'Hey…*

What a wobbly-tobbly walk!' She said,
'Are you sick or something? Dizzy head?'
Oops, Jeffrey Jones re-hit the floor
She laughed until it made her quite sore.

'Get up, get up, you silly old thing
I'm laughing so much, my stomach's gone in!'
'I'm trying, I can't, just look at my feet –
I'll have to roll to the end of the street!'

So, roly-poly spun he-by
Daisy *shrieked* to the heavenly sky
Her laughter echoed round and round
People smiled at the happy sound.

'I'm home' he called in a muddy state
(He saw his dad, as he crashed through the gate)
Jeffrey lay flat, on the garden path
Dad called, *'right… roll on into the bath!'*

THE NAGI NOO

Beneath the wash of the Nagl Noo
That runs gently through the Blim-Le-Woo
Grow water-weeds, that *quiver* and *quob*
And damselflies with silver-wings
They hover, dressed in blue and green.

A precious under-water-view
Beneath the flow of the Nagi Noo
Those water-weeds, they *wift* and *waft*
Midst corrugated, sandy-slopes
Where water-boatmen row and row.

And large-fish dart, like submarines
To lunch? To some fishy-meetings?
On their way, or returning from
I know not where, but do suppose
They know which way they mean to go.

A wasp drinks at the water's edge
Small ripples drift-off to a ledge
Where lichen clings on rotting wood
And aphids climb on nettle leaves
Above an orange centipede.

Beneath the flow of the Nagi Noo
That runs gently through the Blim-Le-Woo
With branches dipping, *splish* and *splash*
Leaning at the water's side
A willow plays with water-sprites.

Sun-rays, long, like golden swords
Shimmering, pulsing, Knighthood-thoughts
Cut the swell of the flowing stream
Sharp as metal, do they appear
I feel, King Arthur's voice is near.

And so, and yes, I'm homeward bound
I stand, my shape left on the ground
Reluctantly, I turn my heels
A robin pipes as I walk on
Through nature's fine, majestic throng.

DOGS AND HUMANS

One dog, two dogs, three dogs, four
And I can count so many more
Pedigrees and multi-breeds
Each one gracing all the trees.

Dogs in the river, dogs on the lead
Dogs barking louder than human's pleas
Humans and dogs, each one with a smile
Sun and the river, we all turn wild.

Exhausted, we get in the car for home
Dog in the back, flat out, flat down
Back home, the human flops in the chair
Flat out, flat down, too tired to care.

FAIRIES

Fairies come to mend the webs
When strong winds blow, or someone treads...
And pulls-apart the shiny threads
Woven there beneath the hedge...

By spider

Fairies call, *'it's all right, we'll weave and sew tonight, tonight'*
Fairies call, *'it's all right, we'll weave and sew tonight, tonight...*

...Ah, ah, ah, ah, ah'

Fairies

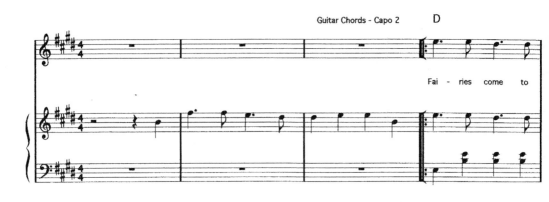

Guitar Chords - Capo 2

D

Fai - ries come to

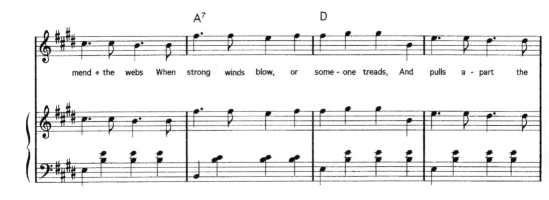

A⁷   D

mend o the webs   When strong winds blow,   or some - one treads,   And pulls a - part the

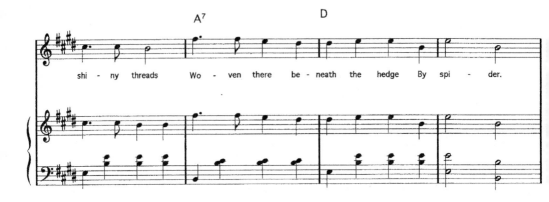

A⁷   D

shi - ny threads   Wo - ven there be - neath the hedge   By spi - der.

Fai - ries call: "It's all right, We'll weave and sew to - night, to - night!"

Fai - ries call: "It's all right, We'll weave and sew to - night, to - night!"

WALKING WITH ELEPHANTS

Put your best foot forward
Keep your eyes well peeled
Watch out! There's an elephant about
...Never tread on her heels!

Lift your spirit upwards
Duck from the swinging trunk
When she calls, *'come walk with me?'*
Say, *'yes I will, what fun!'*

Don't argue with an elephant
They rarely do forget
Be a good companion and
Never speak of vets!

You may well walk for hours
Through bush and briar and mud
When she trumpets, *'this is nice!'*
Don't moan, *'my feet are tired!'*

Be careful with your footsteps
You could get squashed, you might!
Elephant's eyes are really quite small
Compared to their big body size.

So, fling your best foot forward
Keep a cheery grin
Elephants love good company
You could even start to sing

'Tra-la, la-la-la, la, la, la.'

JIMMY HOW YOU JUMP

When Jimmy was a jolly little boy of three
Growing as tall as a tall, tall tree
He was so full of energy

He couldn't sit still on his Papa's knee
He'd learned to walk, he'd learned to talk
He'd learned to *jump* with a *thump, thump, thump...*

Oh, Jimmy how you *jump, jump, jump, jump*
Jimmy how you *jump, jump, jump, jump*
Jimmy how you *jump, jump, jump, jump*

'You remind me of a kangaroo!' Said Mum.

When Jimmy was a jolly little boy of ten
Growing as tall as old Big Ben
With legs as long, as long can be

Captain of the Junior Team was he
Running, jumping round the track
Faster than a bee, with a rocket on its back!

Oh, Jimmy how you *run, run, run, run*
Jimmy how you *run, run, run, run*
Jimmy how you *run, run, run, run*

'You remind me of an antelope!' Said Mum.

When Jimmy was a jolly young lad of twelve
He won a cup and a gold medal
For jumping high and running fast

His *hop-skip-jump*, was quite first class!
His Mother rolled her eyes and smiled
His Father said, *'just look at that child!'*

*Oh, Jimmy how you jump, jump, jump, **jump***
*Jimmy how you run, run, run, **run***
*Jimmy how you hop, **hop-skip-jump***

'You remind me of a frog-on-a-spring!' Said Mum.

TRUM, THE PINK WIND FROM THE ORB OF ORE

I stood there, tense, on the silent hill,
Not a sound could be heard in the air
Even the rabbits had stopped to look
Even the sound of the babbling brook
Seemed to hush, as we heard... *'beware!'*

First a gust, then a billowy whirl
I was blown to one side and I fell
Grabbing on tight to a near-by tree
This wind kept blowing and blowing at me
Then I heard it shout, *'well, well, well...*

I'm Trum, the pink wind, from the Orb of Ore!'

It laughed and blew in my face
I pulled my hat down, stood firm on the ground
Starting to shake, I could feel my heart pound
Down the hill, Trum whooshed and raced.

It blew on the rocks, the trees and flowers
Breaking them all, one by one
Squirrels froze, crows called in vain
Frogs went a-jumping, then jumping again
Badger ran backwards, and thought he was done!

Back Trum came with a whoosh and a snarl
The sound of it hurt my ears
I hunched my shoulders and closed my eyes
I grit my teeth and heaved a sigh...

'I will fill you full of fear...

I can blow windows open, blow windows shut
Break fences and shake up your head
Take your thoughts and make them mine
Rip up the spider webs that I find!'

'You seem horrid! You do!' I said.

'Ha, ha' Trum growled, *'Oh watch me now!'*
It bashed the babbling brook
Most of the fish flipped hither and thither
All of the ducks, they quacked and quivered
It felt like our whole world shook!

Just then, sun called through the stormy clouds
Pointing a golden finger

'Enough, enough of the bad deeds you've done
I've warned you before, now, this sentence has come...
Go now! And do not linger!'

Trum stopped in its tracks, then blew slightly back
Knowing its fate was cemented
Trum had to return to the Great Orb of Ore
Never to leave through the wide-open door
It spat, and then whooshed, quite demented!

I crouched very low as it shot in the air
Cursing and crashing like thunder
There was a loud bang, then Trum disappeared
Taking with it, all of everyone's fears
We were silent and breathless, in wonder!

Spiders re-spun their
webs torn and strewn

Frogs hopped back
and brave birds sang

Badger popped out
of a hole in the ground

Fish relocated and
ducks gathered round

And me... I picked up
my bag and I ran!

19

WALKING WITH HAMSTERS

When walking with a hamster
You need eyes in your feet
Make sure you've tied your laces –
Your socks pulled-up and neat.

Now, be prepared for anything
It might climb up your leg!
It's just no use complaining
A lead won't fit its head.

When walking with a hamster
You must stay on your toes
They tend to change direction
Whichever way you go.

They hardly walk a straight line
For very long at all
More, a *zig-zag-rush-around*
A very puzzling walk!

Turn for just one moment
To chat to mum or dad
Hamsters tend to disappear
And that, is that, is *that*!

You'll end up crawling on your knees
Searching under things
Like, tables, chairs and down the stairs
Even in the bin!

Once I had a hamster –
Crawled through the skirting-board
He found his way to freedom
'Pitter-pat,' under the floor!

'What happened?' You may ask me
Well, I'm very glad to say…
It was a special lump of cheese
That really saved the day.

So, be careful now, with hamsters
Although they're pretty nice
You might well lose your patience
…Maybe once, or maybe twice.

THE STARS, THE MOON AND JASMINE

I'm sitting here with jasmine
And the silver moon above
The nights are getting cold now
So, jasmine bears no flowers.

But I remember summer
As no doubt, you do too
The moon and I, familiar friends
We shared the summer through.

I like to sit here quietly
And dream the whole world sleeps
The stars, the moon, and jasmine
The cat, my chair and... me.

MOAN

There was a young man called Tim
Who wanted to own many things
He bought a car that went, zoom, **zoom, zoom**
He bought a big house, with many rooms
He bought a boat, took it up the river
He bought a restaurant, painted it silver
He was very pleased with the things that he owned
Yet, still, he found plenty of time to moan.

COWBOY

'Well, I'm going fur-a-ride on ma hoss!' Said Frank
'Yep-siree, ah-ha, yep-siree!'

He clipped-clopped, *(pretending)* along the street
Looking stupid *(Jim thought that he did!)*.

'What's a hoss?' Scoffed Jim, chasing on his bike
To Frank, now turning the corner
In the distance he heard a bellowing voice...

'Hang-on! I'll get down and I'll saunter.'

'So, what's this cowboy talk?' Huffed Jim
'You really don't sound quite right!'

*'A saunter's a shuffle that cowboys do...
And a hoss is better than a bike!'*

RHYTHMS AND THE RHYMING

'How do you make a rhyme?' She sighed
Pen in hand, held tightly
The paper blank, she looked my way
I smiled back at her brightly.

'Well… Words are sounds, they skip along
On breezes, dancing briskly
You have to catch them one by one
And write them down quite quickly.

The ones that rhyme, they take your breath
You do know when you've caught one
It is a kind of, sort of…

'Wow'

That makes you feel like jumping!

Some rhyme so well and some just won't
You have to keep on catching
Sometimes you have to let words go
…Wait for a special matching.

Then, of course, it's rhythm time
This is a bit like drumming
Tap your fingers on the desk
To measure what you're writing.

Too short? Too long? You'll know… You will!
As you begin to read it
So then, add words, or take away
A bit like mathematics.

Now, take a walk… Go feed the ducks
Yes, leave your rhyme alone
When you return, refreshed and clear
You'll see what you have sown.

Do not despair and never doubt
The rhythm and the rhyming
Some days words may have passed you by
Tomorrow… You could find them!'

ROOT PEOPLE

Root People
Um-wacka-um
Live in the ground
Tum-tee-tum

Root People
Um-wacka-um
Have *wavy* arms
Tum-tee-tum

Root People
Um-wacka-um
Grow flowers and leaves
Tum-tee-tum

Root People
Um-wacka-um
Have *knobbly* knees
Tum-tee-tum

Root People *Yeah!*

Oh they dance with the breeze,
so *wild* and free
They twist and shout,
when the sun comes out

They shimmy and shine,
when the rain beats down
Those Root People...
Yeah!

Make up your own actions for Root People and have some fun!

ACORN-POD

'Who's that living in yonder hut –
Where the chimney-smoke curls high?'

'Why, it is the old man, Acorn-Pod
And his dog called Apple-Pie!'

'Tell me about the old man'
I asked Elf, curiously
And sat with him on a large toadstool
While he told the tale to me.

'The old man is a mystery
Where he came, from no one knows
Some say he's been there always
And he doesn't plan to go.'

'Always and forever?'
I whispered breathlessly

'That's about the truth of it
So...there it is, you see!'

'That's it? That's it? That's all of it?
You've nothing more to say?'

'This is all I know, to date
Now go, be on your way!'

I jumped down from the toadstool
And started down the track
Then, Elf called out, **'he's got a rat...**
Its name is Apple-Jack!'

MY DOG'S GOT FLEAS

'Where's the dog?'

'I don't know!'

'Well, if he's not in the front room
Not in the back room
And not in the garden…
Then I know where he is!'

'Where mum?'

'On my bed…
And only this morning I saw him
Scratching and scratching his head…
And you know what that means!'

'Fleas mum?'

'Yes!

Here boy, come here!
Did you hear me?
Come down here at once!

If you don't…

You can pack your lead
And pack your bone
And leave home!'

'Oh mum…don't!'

SOMETHING IN THE GARDEN SHED

'There's something in our garden shed
It's had a long journey, that's what it said
…Was yawning loudly, with eyes so red
Yes, four arms waving around its head!'

'Uh huh!' Said mother, ironing.
'What are you doing in my clean kitchen?'

'Mixing popcorn and jam, all up in a tin
And I think I'll take it a milky drink
'The something's supper' - nice, don't you think?'

'Mm!' Said mother, still ironing.
'Goodnight' she whispered later that night
'Sweet dreams, sleep tight, don't let the bugs bite!'

'You don't believe me!' William sighed
'It was hungry you know, but now it's all right!'

'Good' said mother, as she switched off the light.

'You take it breakfast?' William cried
'It comes from Mars, on the furthest side
And lost its way among the stars
It's here on Earth now!' William laughed.

'Yes, yes, in the morning' said mother, yawning.

WHERE THE WEIRD FISH RUN

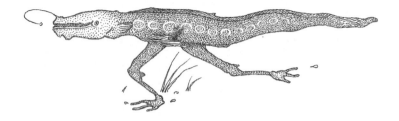

Up early and out, I met Tom, Hugh and Pete
Walking back home from a night-fishing trip
Down by the lake, past the *'Cricketer's Arms'*
The pub on the bend, by the fields and the barns.

They were wiping some wounds with their jumper sleeves
I saw cuts and scratches on their knees
Something had bitten into their clothes
Pete shook his head, and then blew his nose.

'Did you catch any? Many?' I asked, urgently –
Not stopping quite still, I just couldn't you see
I was walking the dog and she pulled me on
With a scent up her nose that seemed to be strong

'Nothing, nothing, not even a bite
But something horrid bit us all right!'
I knew at once, from the sight I could see
Things were very wrong, so I pulled on the lead...

'You've been got by the snappers!' I squealed from the rock
(The rock I stood on, with the sniffing dog)

'That place in the field, by the sandy slope
Hardly anyone now rows there in a boat

Snippy snappy they bite, with teeth sharp and bright
On long leggies they run, at the speed of light
Snippy snappy they bite, from dusk 'till dawn...
Never go when it's dark, they will do you harm!'

'*Oh heavens!*' Cried Hugh, as he winced again
Dabbing the wounds that gave him such pain

'*We were fools to consider it right from the start
I'll never fish there again, in the dark!*'

'*Very wise!*' I said, with my dog in a flurry
I sat on the rock and felt very sorry
I'd heard of these fish from dad and his friends
And this is not where the real story ends…

'*It could have been worse; fingers have been lost
And a few thumbs found, around the rocks!*'
'*Fingers and thumbs?*' Echoed Tom in a panic
Checking his hands and breathing quite badly.

'*Yes… toes as well, from the kicking, you see…
When you kick at those fish, they bite, obviously!
There were toes in the water, bobbing around!*'
…Tom fell with a *plonk*, in a feint, on the ground!

'*Snippy snappy they bite, with teeth sharp and bright
On long leggies they run, at the speed of light
Snippy snappy they bite from dusk 'till dawn…*

Not that way dog! No! Come on… Come on!'

SINBAD THE SPIDER AND FOTHERINGAY, THE FLY

Part 1 - Day Trippers

Sinbad the spider and Fotheringay, the fly
Bumped into each other and both said, *'hi'*...

'What are you up to?' Fotheringay asked

'Spinning a new web' Sinbad gasped...

'If I had wings so fine', he sighed
'To foreign lands I'd surely fly'.

'Well, you've got eight legs' fly beamed back
'That's two more than a fly – a fact!
Think about this special thing
Cheer up now, forget about wings –

It can be tiring, flying! Oui' He said
As he twitched a bit and rolled his head
Then off he flew, *'Adieu, adieu...*
See you spider, well, toodle-oo.'

The fly flew left, he thought that he must
And in through the door of a big yellow bus
He circled the people round and round
Had a merry old time, whizzing up and down.

He stood on their hats, clung to the light
Stared out of the window, he thought that he might
Then, he sat on the bag of Mrs. O' Fah
And sang a few songs as she chatted to Pa.

The bus drove all the way to the coast
The fly had a bird's-eye-view of a boat!
'Smashing', he buzzed as the bus turned round
Revving the engine to drive back to town.

Spider, he'd had a fine day too!
Spun a web on the car of Mrs. Mc Hugh
He'd spun it around the wing mirror's face
And tucked himself in to snooze for the day.

But she'd got in, and driven to France
Boarding the boat with a judder and prance
They sailed the sea, it didn't take long
As quick to cross as a *bang* on a gong.

Down through the streets on yonder shore
Spider held tight to the speeding door
They ended up in a little café
Where they spent the most, of the rest of the day.

So, it was time for home again
The boat, then down the country lanes
She parked with a skid by the acorn tree
'Home safe!' Sinbad sighed, with great relief.

All in all, they hadn't been long
As quick, perhaps, as that bang on a gong.
'I've been to France', spider whistled, *'Cool!'*
As Fotheringay fly flew over the wall.

'And I've been all the way to the coast!'
Said Fotheringay, (not wanting to boast)
'Ha-ha, hee-hee, such travellers are we…
Come on, let's go tell Barbra the Bee!'

Part 2 – Barbra the Bee

Barbra was singing a buzzing song
The chorus was short, but the verses were long
Flying around from flower to flower
Humming the tune, for hours and hours.

Pollen of gold, under tummy and thighs
Pollen from flowers, to take to the hive
'Be quiet! Hush up!' croaked a croaky old frog
With fingers in ears, on a near-by log.

'What a noise, little bee!' cried a passing snail
To Barbra, whose song had now pitched to a wail
But her favourite tune just had to be sung
From beginning to end, until it was done!

So, Barbra flew high in the mulberry tree
Whilst brushing some pollen away from her knee
She soared high above, looked down at the pair
Then her voice was heard, floating through the air...

'I'm sorry!' she called, *'my apologies...
I'll finish the verses up here in this tree
If you don't like the song, I can see how it might
Give a headache or two – so maybe you're right...*

*Up here I'll stay 'till I meet my friends
I've work to do, and then honey to blend!'.*
She stuck her head into another flower
And sang the next song for a further hour.

Fotheringay buzzed-round a dustbin he'd found
Waiting for Sinbad to crawl over-ground
Crawling and flying are two different things
(It's faster we know, when flying with wings.)

Bee heard the sound of her friend, the fly
So, she put her breaks on, way up in the sky
Then dived *whoosh* – down to the dustbin lid
With a *ping* and a *ding* and a *squeaky skid.*

Walking his way over bush, brick and flower
Spider arrived within half an hour
The three sat there in the warm, evening sun
And Barbra laughed, *'well, what have you done?'*

'We've come to tell of our travelling day'
Wheezed spider, *'And... I wanted to say...*
*It's been great! I don't know **where** to begin'*
So, the fly, then told the tale for him...

'He's been to France. I went to the coast!'
Fly spoke of the boat *(not wanting to boast!)*
'Well, well,' hummed Barbra, buzzing around
(She was far too buzzy to sit for long.)

'I'm all amazed, I am indeed
*I've never, **ever** seen the sea!'*
'Then come with us next time!' They cried
'A fabulous trio, bee, spider and fly!'

They said *'Toodle-oo'* and all shook hands
With *great* expectations of foreign lands
'It's something to sleep on!' Barbra-bee said
As she finished her song *just* in time for bed.

JOSHUA'S SECRET JUNGLE LAND

Joshua's secret jungle land
Is quite a special tale, you know
(I only tell you in this rhyme
Because you know a friend of mine)
Others search, but never find
This land that has no place in time.

Joshua's secret jungle land
Is wholly straight, yet sometimes round
Depending on which way you stand
And where you point whichever hand
Now watch the wind, see where it blows
This is the way you have to go!

Joshua's secret jungle land
Has many of my friends encamped
In places hid behind the boughs –
Of trees, or heard, among the flowers
Quite lost before your eyes, until
You walk a circle round the hill.

Joshua's secret jungle land
Is bright and clear, most of the year
But Thursdays, when the moon is high
There is a mist which spreads and hides
The trees and animals from sight
Unless, you sneeze and blink twice.

To find this place, you read this rhyme
And follow the words, in which you'll find
The secret way, the only way
And may you find it, 'yes' I say
So, if you do, and should you dare
Look out for me, I'll see you there.

HUBBLE BUBBLE GONE

Hubble bubble pops and stinks
Manifesting from the sink
Tom and John just back from school
Playing wizards, mixing gruel

A bit of this, a cup of that
Some magic words, that Tom made up
'Ho, this is an awful pong!'

'Yes, it's great! Just carry on!'

Heating up upon the stove
Simmering odours up their noses
John's eyes rolled his throat then swelled
He couldn't take the wretched spell

In fact, he then was seeing double
From the waft that shook and bubbled
'I think this is enough of that!'
John said, with his face screwed up.

They tried to pour it down the drain
No one heard their wild refrain…
'Help!' They called and called again
But stuck to it they did remain!

Sticky it was, very sticky
The green bits, particularly
Dragged and screaming, down the drain
Never to be seen again… *never to be seen again…*

Gone!

THE DAUGHTERS AND THE SONS

I heard the word from a singing bird
Nestled in the branches
We talked of June and the coming moon
And other little matters.

The breeze, breezed by and winked its eye
It rustled the red tulips
The colour swirled around my mind
To when, last time, I knew you.

I listened well, I heard the tale
Of ancient walls and sanskrit
I touched my toe, I touched my nose
To check if I was sleeping.

The bird above, became a dove
It dropped me down, a feather
Telling me to keep it safe
To wrap it up in heather.

The hot-sun danced-round and around
The pond it turned to glitter
A dragonfly, it settled-down
I watched its very wonder.

A toad and then, a grasshopper
Jumped, laughing, in the daisies
I felt that I had learned a lot
Although the day was hazy.

Come dance around the Rowan tree
We'll sing up to the sun
The deer, the lamb, will gather here
Their eyes will shine with love.

'So, bring your hearts, yes everyone –
Come circle,' spoke the one

'The dove will sing a sacred song, for
The daughters, and the sons.'

WALKING WITH SNAILS

I really did get soaked that day
All in all, sploshed to the skin
When first we began our little walk
Sun was out and beaming beams.

The plan was to take a gentle stroll
With Sidney snail, and muse
We started off at 8:00am
By lunch we'd hardly moved!

Then rain, it fell, a mighty fall
Leaves dripped, oh how they dripped!
The water-barrel, fit to burst
And puddles became deep…

Deep enough to flow-in shoes
I wasn't dressed for rain
My Wellies, they were in the shed
I thought, 'oh what a pain!'.

Sidney was all-right, of course
Inside his shell, tucked in
He didn't mind the rain that much
But I had squeaky skin.

He then slid up a peony
And chomped upon a leaf
I didn't fancy leaves for lunch
I much prefer fried squid.

When I survey the length of it
We walked two metres flat
Well, snails don't walk, they slide of course
So, be prepared for that!

A CHAT WITH MY CAT

Tortoiseshell cat, on top of the wall
A scratch on his nose, from a fight at dawn
Now, yawning and lazy, but last night half crazy...
Such spits and howls on the lawn!

'No, don't smile at me! You don't fool me you see
With your purring and cleaning your paws
You fought like a wild cat! No, not like a nice cat
I'm shocked at the sight that I saw!

Oh, now you want breakfast and maybe a long nap?
Shall we call this recovery?
You were nice when I bought you, what have I taught you?
Be kind to your friends on this street!

I see you are smiling - I'm not happy, Thomas!
I'll finish this nice cup of tea
And wait for a 'sorry' regarding this folly
You truly embarrass me!

Mrs. Brown might well have a word to say
When she sees the state of her cat
Oh... you didn't start it; you didn't spit first!
Hmm... are you so sure about that?

I know what I saw and I know what I heard
So...inside now, through that front door!
You'll stay in my sight. Yes, you'll stay in all night
And tomorrow, you'll shake ginger's paw!

Did you hear?
Tomorrow, you'll shake Ginger's paw!'

'Meow'

39

SILLY WORDS

Quiggerly, quaggerly, quimpilly quoob

Here are four silly words, just for you

If it's raining, you're waiting

Or can't get to sleep

This is much better than counting sheep

Squartle, squiggle, squibbery, squooj

Make up silly words

Its such good fun to do!

STORM IN A TEACUP

This teacup must be a magical cup
Oh yes, it really must be!
For out of it flew a hundred or more
Of the most, peculiar things.

And stormy, describes the voice that I heard…
The voice that bellowed within
Odd things flew out, at a pace quite wild
All in all, such a horrible din!

'Get out!' It cried, *'be off with you now!'*
And out flew the Jack of Hearts
Shortly to follow, the shocked Queen of Clubs
Then, the rest of the pack, of the cards.

'Skedaddle, scoot! Get out of my way!'
Screamed the voice, and then, yet again…
Out sped a clock and a frightened sock
A doll and an old metal train.

'No more! Be gone! I'll not carry on!'
Out shot a spoon, a fork and a knife
A unicorn ducked, as it spun past a jug
Followed by, old King Cole's wife.

'Leave my teacup! Vamoose, off you go!'
The voice was now verging on rage
I never found out, what the noise was about
Not then, not now… to this day!

THE DAY OF DELIGHT

I wonder who actually thought of it first?
But then, does it really matter?
I know the forest was fit to burst
With squeals, with joy and with laughter.

Invitations were sent to everyone
Not a single someone was left out

Even Liam, the cheeky leprechaun
Though some did have their doubts!

This could be the best party ever
With dancing, into the night
A gathering of all the forest folk
Celebrating, *'The Day of Delight.'*

The day arrived, that special day
It was August the thirty-second
Everyone got up early to help
To be there for the preparations.

At 3:88 By the crazy clock
Sweet music began to play
Three by two they all arrived
On a gloriously, sunny day.

They drank daisy tea with honey
From daisy-petal cups
Kindly poured by bumble-bee
I think she had the hiccups!

Edward, the smart tin soldier
Took his sword to cut the cake
And Mutt, the wise magician
Gave them plates that would not break.

Pearly, the shiny salmon jumped –
With a spin, in the near-by stream
Calling, *'hey, hey, this is fun!'*
'Oh, yes!' They all agreed!

Milkshake from the strawberry stream
Was the pinkest-treat to drink
But Liam the cheeky leprechaun
Stole the straws, with a laugh and a wink.

Geronimo, the kindly giant
As tall as the aspen tree
Called, *'Liam put them back now!'*
Liam did, immediately!

Wicked Wanda, the party-pooper
Her head full of dreadful deeds
Tripped on her long, long fingernails –
Rolled into the water weeds

Help came again
from Geronimo
He bent down
upon his knees
She thanked him
with a smiling-frown
…Not used to
caring deeds.

Tasty chocolate sandwiches –
Stacked, tall as a mountain high
We couldn't see above them
And I think they touched the sky!

Everyone looked so delightful
Wearing bluebells from woody-dell
They all had a party present
A wish, from the wishing well.

Handel's Water Music
Was played by the running-stream
The rainbow-jellies jiggled
In time to a tambourine.

Then, Sweetie, the silver ladybird
Screamed out a painful, *'ouch!'*
It was Liam sitting next to her
Someone gave him quite a shout!

Glow-worms lit up the pathway
Into the fading light
One by one the children slept
While toadstools sang, *'goodnight.'*

The Queen of Fairies waved her wand

'I'd like to make a toast —
Peace and happiness forever
To all the forest folk!'

'Hurrah' they cheered, *'Hurrah*
And so, say all of us
Peace and happiness forever'
(Wicked Wanda huffed!)

What a time, such a special time
They danced into the night
The best tea party ever...
Yes, on this, *'the Day of Delight'*.

JO'S FIVE CATS

Casper ran upstairs, we made some tea
Then we heard a shocking *spit*
The sort of sound that cats make
When they are not too pleased.

Then, a *'thud'* on the floor above
And a *thump, thumpity-thump.*
Down comes Nellie to join us
It looked like she'd had a bump.

'What's up Nellie? Had a fight?
That Casper's a naughty lad!
You should really know by now
Come here, it'll be alright'.

Three-legged Nellie, sat on the mat
And then, she *spat* at me!
She did look in a foul mood
As we sat and drank our tea.

Sweet Suzi-Kettles, with her big tum
Purred and pawed on my jeans
Looked at one-eyed Nelson
Then stuck three claws in me!

Hamish-The-Brave, as shiny as coal
In his handsome, well-cleaned coat
Winked, then yawned, as Nellie growled
Somewhere deep in her throat.

I thought we'd have a little fun
With a paper-ball and string
Not one cat cared to move at all
This seemed a funny thing!

Jo laughed, of course she had a plan
A trick to change their mood...
Biscuits! Wow! The five cats, jumped -
And danced, to the sound of food.

TIME AND TIME AGAIN

Time is a funny thing you know
The more it comes, the more it goes
Take for instance, 'yesterday'
Well, that was once, 'today'.

The more it goes, the more it comes
Like distant tapping on a drum
A pendulum, a boomerang
A tiresome wait, a wonderland.

How did time start? Where does it end?
This could drive me round the bend!
I really, sometimes, get confused
Is it me? Or do you too?

I sometimes think that space and time
Are really kinds of *'other lands'*
Magic worlds, in which to be
To learn the things, we really need.

To get things wrong, seems quite alright
There is more time to set our sights
So many things to find and learn
And through it all, the clock still turns.

Why does it turn? What does it count?
I've never, really worked this out
Perhaps it's just so I can see
That I am never late for tea!

LITTLE LUCY MINNIE LOCKET

Little Lucy Minnie Locket
Liked to sit in dad's coat pocket
When she first came to our house
Hardly bigger than a mouse
Fluffy, warm, and sort of brown
She could curl in my mum's hands!

Little Lucy Minnie Locket
Came to me on my fifth birthday
It was such a big surprise
Looking up with shiny eyes
I asked my mum, *'whose dog is that?'*
She said, *'it's yours!'* I jumped and clapped!

My lovely Little Lucy Locket
Kiss, kiss, lots of kisses
Just sometimes she bites my nose
It's her way of saying *'hello'*
She gets caught in my mum's feet
All my friends think she's so sweet.

Little Lucy Minnie Locket
Loves to walk, while we go shopping
A pink ribbon in her hair
Even boys bend down to greet her!
I'd have thought they'd call her *'stupid'*
But they say, *'she's so cute!'*... Lucy...

Yes, I'd have thought they'd call her *'stupid'*-
But they say, *'she's so cute!'* Lucy.

WALKING WITH CRABS

'Walking with crabs!' (You shout to me)
'Yes, I know, it's quite absurd!
Well, you probably need to be on a beach
To appreciate my words, and…

Wear strong shoes, when on your walks
Don't arrive with just bare toes
They can pack-a-pinch, from their beaky-claws
Oh, oh! If they do use those!

To walk with crabs, you must be brave
Enquire where they wish to go?
Is it backwards? Sideways? Round again?
Bend down and say, **'hello!'**

'When do you get to here?' (I point) –
'To where I'd like you to be
The opposite direction (I point)
Is the long-way-round you see!'

'Talking to me? Hmm!' Asked the crab
'Yes, yes, to you, I speak…
Will you walk this way, just over here –
Or will it take a week?'

Well… the only consolation is
It depends who you're talking to
Walk with a crab who's interesting
Could be a plus for you.

You could learn of the sea, know of the tides
Discover the shrimps and whelks
Ask of the rocks, where his family live – and
What are his favourite shells?

So maybe you won't even get to there –
To where you do hope to go
But, inspiring conversation
Could make up for it, you know!

SLIPS AND LADDERS

Sarah stood on the head of her bed
To reach the book above the egg
Given to her last Easter time
It still looked very, very nice!

Well, back to the book…

The book fell down into the tank
The fish freaked out and out they jumped
Into the air, then down on the chest
The old pine chest for socks and vests.

Well, over to the cat…

The cat perked up and gave a smile
Fish became lunch! 'Meow, meow'
Cat then sat on the brand, new rug
A very fine rug from Alice and Doug.

Well, back to Sarah…

Sarah had stood precariously
Feet had slipped from the bed-head you see
She then '*flew*' with shrieks, to the floor
A lovely green floor, matching the door.

Well, over to you…

What do you think? A really wrong move?
Don't balance like that! Oh, please, never do!
She did end up with a broken toe
I'm sorry to say, but there you go!

She learned her lesson sure and true
Get a ladder and always think it through!

THE LYCHEE, THE AVOCADO AND ME

When I was young, well… probably three
Mum planted an avocado seed
Now I'm seven, and here's the truth…
There's a tree in our living room!

Although I'm growing, it's taller than me
Funny how seeds turn into a tree!

Last month, we planted a lychee seed
I'm waiting, waiting, waiting to see!
The seed has opened, there is a white root
To follow that, there should be a shoot.

I was thinking…

There won't be much room to watch TV
With so many branches, and hundreds of leaves
Would I even be able, to find a seat?
With the lychee, the avocado and me.

BEING FRANK

Well, I'm just going to be frank
And that is that!
Yes, I know there's work to be done
But I must have some day-dream-fun...

Such as...

Balancing tea-cups on the dog
Singing a duet with a frog
Fishing for shrimps
And talking to newts
Dancing a jig
Wearing Wellington boots

And that's not all...

Riding an elephant
On heathered moors
Laughing and laughing
Sleigh-rides at dawn
Liquorice-all-sorts
Stuck on my nose

Sing, *'hallelujah'*
Up on tip-toes

Thunder striking –
Chords-cross-the-sky
Swans low-flying
Oh, such a sight

Hollering **loud**
On the Norfolk Broads
Simply being
Out of doors

I know that study, I must, indeed
But, give me some moments to day-dream...

Please!

AUNTIE VERA

Auntie Vera's ill in bed
Face all white, her nose is red
Sneezing, coughing, a little bit sharp
I'd better be quiet for a start!

Auntie Vera's ill in bed
Somethings banging in her head
Box of tissues and two white pills
Yes, she's caught a very bad chill.

Auntie Vera's ill in bed
'Better stop jumping!' Mummy said
'I know she's grumpy, but she's in pain
Soon, she will be well again!'

THE MINIMS

The Minims live in a lovely place,
Called Nimony Avenue
Minims have a lot of hair and they all play violins too!
They sleep in houses round and stubby
Built with circular stones
Each garden has a string-a-ling tree and a kitten of its own.

With manuscript paper and inky pens
They write musical notes most days
Composing melodic, heavenly sounds
That can waft you up and away.
I would have to say they are gifted, yes, this I would have to say
Sometimes I sit for hours and hours just to hear them play.

There's a doctor, a baker, a violin maker
A pet shop, a vet and a bank
The music shop is a busy place, it's the busiest shop in town!
With trees, kittens and lavender fields –
Some swings for the children to play
I would have to say, I like to be there. I try to pop in most days.

The only human there abouts, is a boy called, Timothy Bright
He lights the street lamps, three by two –
Precisely, every night.
Yes, three by two and up and down
When night tucks in the town, he
Sprightly climbs, with a precious flame, so the Minims won't fall down.

For when it's dark, they could trip and fall, or step upon a kitten!
An important job for Timothy Bright
The Minims really, love him.
So let me take you further on, as
There's more for us to see
I'll take you to the station. It's this way, One... Two... Three...

Here's the happy station, one train arrives each week
It always carries kisses, and
They land upon your cheek.
You must be good-as-gold of course
At least, have really tried
If not, ah-well, it seems to be, those kisses fly on by!

Well, it's time for me to go right now. I'll say, 'bye-bye' to you
I hope you have enjoyed yourself
At Nimony Avenue.
Perhaps we can come back again?
We might, we may, we will!
Next time, ah yes, let's dance with them, and hug a kitten too!

WALKING WITH DOGS

Walking with dogs, laughing with dogs
It's the best! Oh yes, is it not!
A friend for life, there by your side
Eyes all-aglow, ears reaching high
Loyal and loving, wanting kind words
And giving all that she's got.

Hope for a run, a hug and some food
With eyes that speak mountains to you
It doesn't need words to know what she wants
You and your friend have your own tête-à-tête
After time, you can read her mind too.

Out in the wind, the rain and the snow
In the sun 'neath the skies so blue
We're out in it all, with our coat and strong shoes
Slipping and *sliding*, *dancing* and *gliding*
Sometimes in Wellingtons too!

A cuddle on the couch, a snooze on the bed
Dog hairs and mud, quite expected
In and under, a snuggle-warm cover
Rolling and *barking*, *snuffling* and *snorting*
Oi! snorting is just not accepted!

And so, we sleep, its cosy and warm
My dearest canine and me
I'm dreaming of scones and hot, steaming tea
She might be dreaming of chicken and peas
And a bone, when her bowl becomes empty.

LIZARDS

Dad bought two lizards, in a tank

Ugh!

One was jumpy and actually jumped!

Ugh!

The other was quiet and stared at me
I couldn't eat lunch; I couldn't eat tea!
He said he might go back for a snake

Oh yuck!

This thought could easily keep me awake

YUCK!

It's been such an awful, terrible day
I think I might have to move away!

JOHANNA'S JUMP

'I'm two years and one month
Look, I've just learned to jump!
It took many tries, again and again -
For my feet to leave the ground.

I've tried, I have, so very hard
Now I can do it more
There's just one thing, my knees won't bend
I do crash on the floor!

How can I get my knees to bend?
Must I tell my brain?
I'll close my eyes and take a breath
And try it once again.

I'll get it right. I will quite soon
And learn just what to do
Yes, my name is Johanna and
I've just turned two!'

NOSE TO NOSE WITH A RODENT (RATS)

I placed the cage upon the bed
Where mother was a-snoozing
It was a July afternoon
I think, about four-thirty.

'Oh!' She said, as she turned her head
Nose-to-nose with a rodent
'Summer holidays mum,' I said
'No-one there to feed them!'

Six weeks later, and back to school
My mother said, *'I'll miss them!'*
She squeaked her lips and scratched their heads –
'Goodbye Tom and Susan!'

THE LITTLE BROKEN CAR

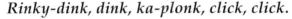

The little car had a broken door
It made a noise, as it fell on the floor
It made a noise, something like this…
Rinky-dink, dink, ka-plonk, click, click.

The little car had a broken exhaust
It made a noise, yes it did of course!
It made a noise, something like this…
Rinky, bang, bang, chugga-whomp, whizz-bang!

The little car had a broken wheel
It made a noise like the rubbing of steel
It made a noise, something like this…
Rinky, scratch, scratch, wobble-whomp, dink, dink.

The little car had a broken spring
It made a noise like a squeaky tin
It made a noise, something like this
Rinky, ping, ping, burp-whomp, squeak, squeak.

'Can you fix it please?' Asked Sophie Smith's dad
'I can indeed!' Said the garage-man.
'Any idea how much will it be?
'I'd better find out…just one minute please!'

So, he scratched his head, and began to write.
Little-car looked; its eyes shining bright
As the garage-man said, *'I know, I know -*
It'll cost, two balloons and a jelly-ice!'

'Oh', said Sophie Smith…
   'that's grand! What's your name,
   Mr. Garage Man?'

   'Why, it's Jasper B –
  that's J and a B
 We'll fix your car,
  *in a **clickety-click**'.*

≪ ≪ ≪ First left to Jasper's garage

BEANS

Beans on my bacon
Beans on my eggs
Whenever I'm asked
I always say, *'yes!'*

Beans with my toasties
Beans with my chops
It's hard to say no
I like beans so much.

Beans on fresh custard
Beans with old cheese
One day I even
Had beans on my knees!

THE HURRAH POEM

The kettle of Baldocka
It was quite a whopper
Could fill 200 cups, in one go
200 Cups of hot, steaming tea
All from one fill, don't you know!

No-one could lift it
Well, not from this planet
So they all had to wait for tea
Wait for the giant from Bodly-Odd
To arrive, at best, in a week!

Hurrah for the giant
From Bodly-Odd
Hurrah for her towering strength
Hurrah for the tea, hurrah indeed!
Another cup, if you please!

THOUGHTS ON WORMS

Thought I'd collect some worms today
It just came into my mind
I stood there in the pouring rain –
Now, how many can I find?

I dug with a spoon, my best, best spoon
My knees got covered in mud
I didn't know where to put them all
So, decided then, to stop.

Another thought came into my head
As the rain *'tip-tapped'*, *'tip-tapped'*
Somewhere, I knew, in the garden shed
Was my nice, new, pink handbag.

So, up-on-toes, I got it down
Shiny-pink, with a golden clip
I put the worms in, one by one
Making sure that they did fit.

Rain beat hard, on the roof of the shed
Worms wiggled and they squiggled
Rain ran down the hair on my head
And I began to giggle.

Mum told me straight, to put them back
She said, *'this isn't clever!'*
I did agree and put them back
To make them all feel better.

MACKINDA MACKADA MACKOO

In the town of Mackinda Mackada Mackoo
There was a noisy hullabaloo
Word got out, spread far and wide
Folks said, *'oh, what a to-do!'*

Well, I'd better tell you the reason why...
Should I? Dare I? Do you want to know?
Are you sure? Very sure? Hmm, is that so?
Well, here it is, and here we go...

I'll tell you, in case you go that way
You might even plan to go today!
See... Mackinda folk like to make you jump
They shout, **'boo'** to whatever you say!

Yes, of course you're startled! Of course, you jump!
The shock, it has great effect
Ask a policeman the way. *'First left, **boo'***
It's hardly what you would expect!

It's true, quite soon, you know the score
You find you don't' jump, you just scream!
With the boo's and the screaming, spoiling the days
Visitors rarely were seen.

Now, a girl called Veranda, with sticky-up-hair
Said, *'I know how to stop this racket!'*
She sat thinking, hard, in her thinking-school-chair
Her teacher said, **'boo, be quiet!'**

Next morning was free, there was no school
So, Veranda went marching to town
And before a Mackina could shout the word, **'boo'**
She turned and she stuck out her tongue!

She visited every shop in sight
Every house, in fact, everyone!
Her tongue stuck out a hundred times
Until she was really quite tired.

The town was shocked, they seemed to forget
Forgotten, *vamoosed*, all gone!
The Mackinda folk went quietly about
Veranda's idea, it had won!

There's no-one left at all today
Who remembers the word we won't say!
It's peaceful, no more hullabaloo
Now, Mackinda's a very nice place.

Oh, just a few words of precaution perhaps
For those who might feel so inclined…
Sticking your tongue out at other folk
Is **not** the done – thing, I find!

A PAGE TO COLOUR IN:

CATCH A STICKLEBACK

Catching sticklebacks with your hands
Can you, do it? See if you can
Though you think it may be easy
I've tried, in fact, it's very tricky

Splash...

oops...missed again!

Just make sure, you don't fall in
We must be careful, pond or stream
Now, keep your hands cupped quietly
All of your fingers shut, tightly

Splash...

oops...missed again!

Oh, no, don't make a sudden move
The fish will dive away from you
Wait, let them swim up very near
Keep the water still and clear...

Then catch...

my word! You've got one!

THE BORING GHOST

Out jumped a ghost, face whiter than white
As Mimi came down for a drink in the night
With shock and surprise, ghost popped its eyes
And completely forgot to say, *'boo'*.

Ghost was confused, and started to twitch
You see, Mimi just couldn't be bothered with it
'I had planned to say boo and frighten you -
I see you prefer to walk past me!

You're supposed to be scared
and run off somewhere

Scream
'Ghost in my house,'
from the top of the stairs

Or faint on the floor…
hide behind a closed door

This is bad for my
ghost reputation!'

'Sorry', she said with a mighty big yawn
'But I do find you totally boring'
She clapped her hands and then rattled some pans
Ghost sped to a corner shaking.

'Well, I'm back off to bed now!' Mimi said
While scratching an itch on her forehead
'If you're still here at three, do make us some tea…
I'll take mine with some milk and no sugar.'

THE ANTIQUE SHOP

I need a run up to the park
I've got to *jump*, I've got to *bark* – woof*!*
Spin-around, be up-side-down

Stretch my legs and chase the swans
All day I've sat here on the floor
Just waiting to get *out* the door!

Mum, take us to the park, the swings
Let's feed the squirrels, have ice-cream
All day it's been,

don't touch, don't touch

Why can't I ride the rocking horse?
The dog and I, we've had enough
Of serving in the antique shop!

From ten this morning, 'til six tonight
We've watched the people walking past
Some come to look, some come to buy

Some chat and chat to pass the time
I've drawn three pictures, looked-around
And you just say,

sit down, sit down!

I've polished a table, cleaned a chest
I found some woodworm and a scratch
A lovely painting, a nasty sketch

An alligator! Is it dead?
Tick-tock, the clock goes round and round
Oh mum, enough, the park,

the park!

THE MILKWOOD DRAGON

I've heard many a story of the Milkwood Dragon
Many a tale of its fiery nose
Seen many-a picture of the Milkwood Dragon
But I *never, ever* saw it alive, myself…

Um-tra-la la, la, loddle - liddle-lom

I've heard many a song about the Milkwood Dragon
Sung quite loud, from north to south
My friend Paul, says he's seen this dragon
But I *never, ever* saw it alive, myself…

Um- tra-la, la la, loddle- liddle-lom

I'll draw you a picture of the Milkwood Dragon
I'll sketch it now, from top to toe
If you ever, *ever,* ***ever*** meet this dragon
Won't you write me a note, and let me know.

ABRACADABRA

Abracadabra sombrero red
Twenty crocodiles asleep in my bed
Two hundred judges wearing wigs
Two thousand horses dancing a jig
Two big helpings of custard and figs.

Abracadabra sombrero blue
Forty mice sing to a kangaroo
Four hundred soldiers ambush a cheese
Four thousand fish jump out of the sea
Four currant buns for you and me.

Abracadabra sombrero gold
Sixty elephants feeling the cold
Six hundred auctions and everything sold
Six thousand bus stops all over the world
Six jelly mountains with creamy whirls.

Abracadabra sombrero brown
Eighty frogs on a merry-go-round
Eight hundred snakes play chess in the sun
Eight thousand lions with tickly tums
Eight gingerbread-men get up and run.

Abracadabra sombrero black
One hundred dogs with cricket bats
One thousand chips in a frying pan
One million magicians shout out, *'shazam!'*
And ten big spoons of strawberry jam.

ACKNOWLEDGEMENTS

Thank you to each of the illustrators: Soledad Echarte, Steve Lancaster, James McKay and Quin Rice; gifted people I met over different periods of time. Thank you for bringing the descriptions of the characters, to life. I found it thrilling to see them on the page!

As decades have passed, I now need to say that Quin Rice is no longer with us. I miss you, my good friend; thank you for your lovely artwork.

Thank you to Joan Rambridge for the early editing of some of this work in 1999. Your patience and clarity, gave me a boost, to continue on brightly with the project. Thank you also, for your story which inspired me to write the Minims.

Thank you to Alison Wren for your graphic design work and speed in getting the manuscript into shape. It brought me a lot of joy to see the first draft. Thank you for your support; you shone a light of hope at a very good time.

Thank you to Gill Evans and to Kate Dossett. I ambushed you out of the blue, and asked you to consider reading the draft. Happily, you did! It has been very much appreciated. Some of your comments are on the back cover.

The 'Snow Beach' logo was designed in 2007 by Ed Hopewell-Ash, from a photo of my dog Izzy (a whippet). Ed, I would like to acknowledge and thank you for this logo.

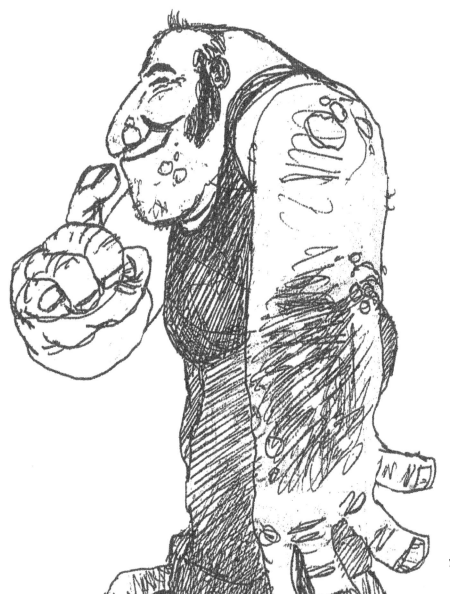

INDEX OF ILLUSTRATORS

AUTHOR'S NOTE

Much of this work is inspired by memories of my childhood in the 1950s and the years when my daughter was growing up in the 1980s. Walks in nature, along the sea-shore, through woodlands and around lakes with my dog, Izzy, gave me further inspiration for storylines.

I was bitten by the writing bug around the age of seven. Together with a passion for painting and nature, I lost myself in the hobbies I loved.

In my early teens, having been drawn to music, I turned my hand to song writing and this then took me onto a professional career in music which lasted some decades.

It has taken me some years to present an actual book. I'm happy to say that the ideas, collected over time, are now gathered together on the pages here. I really enjoyed writing them.

I do hope 'The Day of Delight' brings you miles of smiles.

Marian Moxham

Marian's music began in the late 60s, with the stage name 'Marian Segal'.
Catch Marian's music at: **mariannesegal-jade.com**

Printed in Great Britain
by Amazon

78847408R00047